Billie B. Brown

www.BillieBBrownBooks.com

# Billie B. Brown Books

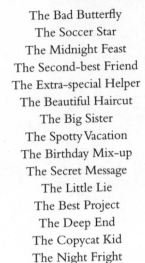

First American Edition 2014
Kane Miller, A Division of EDC Publishing

Text copyright © 2011 Sally Rippin
Illustrations copyright © 2011 Aki Fukuoka
Logo and design copyright © 2011 Hardie Grant Egmont

First published in Australia in 2011 by Hardie Grant Egmont

For information contact:
Kane Miller, A Division of EDC Publishing
P.O. Box 470663
Tulsa, OK 74147-0663
www.kanemiller.com
www.edcpub.com
www.usbornebooksandmore.com

Library of Congress Control Number: 2013944866

Printed and bound in the United States of America
7 8 9 10
ISBN: 978-1-61067-258-0

# The Best Project

By Sally Rippin

Illustrated by Aki Fukuoka

**Kane Miller**
A DIVISION OF EDC PUBLISHING

# Chapter One

Billie B. Brown has twenty-seven popsicle sticks, twelve pipe cleaners and one glue stick. Do you know what the "B" in Billie B. Brown stands for?

# Busy!

Billie is very busy today. She has homework! She is making a tower for her school project.

Billie's teacher is away all week. Another teacher is substituting in Billie's class. Her name is Miss Swan. She wears long skirts and lots of silver bracelets.

Twelve
pipe cleaners

One glue stick

Twenty-seven
popsicle sticks

3

When Miss Swan walks, her skirts go **swish**, **swish**, **swish**. Her bracelets go **jingle**, **jingle**, **jingle**. Billie thinks she is wonderful.

Miss Swan has decided that Billie's class will build a model city. Everyone in the class will make something to put in it.

4

Some kids are making boring things like hospitals or schools. But not Billie. She is making a tower.

But Billie is having a lot of trouble getting her tower to stay up. It wibbles and wobbles, and then it falls down. Billie is beginning to feel very **cross**.

"Stupid tower!" she says.

She throws the glue stick
across the room.

"Billie!" says her mom.
"We don't throw things
in the house."

"Why don't you try something simpler?" says her dad. "You could use a box, like Jack did."

Jack is Billie's best friend. He lives next door. Billie and Jack are in the same class at school. Jack finished his project yesterday. He has made a house out of a box.

It has windows and doors
that open and close.

But Billie doesn't want to
make a boring old house.
She wants to make a
fancy tower.

She feels so **angry** that her head is fizzing.

"I hate this stupid project!" Billie shouts. "My tower will never be ready for school tomorrow!"
She runs upstairs and flops down on her bed.

# Chapter Two

There is a knock on Billie's bedroom door. Her dad comes in. Billie buries her face in the pillow. She wants her dad to know that she is really, really **cross**.

"Hey, Billie," says her dad, patting her head. "Come on. I'll help you build your tower. You just need some stronger glue, that's all."

"All right," says Billie in a **grumpy** voice. But secretly she feels a little better.

Billie and her dad go downstairs to build her tower. Strong glue is too dangerous for Billie to use on her own. So she holds the sticks and her dad glues them together.

Soon the tower is finished. It looks amazing! Billie feels very **proud**. She is sure it will be the best project in the class.

Usually Lola is the best at school projects. But Lola is only making a hospital. Billie has made a tower!

Billie hopes so much that Miss Swan will like her tower. She hopes Miss Swan will put her tower right in the middle of their city.

"What a beautiful tower, Billie!" says her mom. "You'd better put it up on the dining table. You don't want Noah getting hold of it!"

Billie frowns. Babies can be so annoying sometimes. Especially when they start crawling. Noah gets into everything!

"I can't move it yet," says Billie. "It still has to dry."

"Why don't you get ready for bed first?" says her dad. "Then you can come back and move it. It will be dry by then."

"OK," says Billie, yawning. She has been working on her project all evening and now it is late.

Billie puts on her pajamas
and brushes her teeth.
Her dad comes upstairs
to tuck her in. Her mom
is putting Noah to bed.

"Have you moved your
tower?" asks her dad.

"Just going now," says Billie. She runs down to the family room. But her tower is still wobbly. She doesn't want to move it yet. It might fall to pieces again.

Billie decides she will come back later. She can creep downstairs after her dad has read her a story.

Billie's dad tucks her in. He reads her a book about a little girl who lives in Paris. Billie's dad tells Billie that Paris is a big city in France.

The little girl in the book walks her dog through a park full of statues and sculptures. Billie loves this book.

The pictures of Paris are very beautiful.

Billie falls asleep dreaming of the wonderful city her class is going to make with Miss Swan.

Uh-oh...

Billie has forgotten to do something very important.

# Can you remember what it is?

# Chapter Three

The next morning Billie finds it hard to wake up.

"Billie," her mom calls. "Hurry and come down for breakfast. You'll be late for school!"

Billie is feeling very **sleepy**. She pulls on her clothes and goes downstairs for breakfast. Her dad pours some milk on her cereal.

Suddenly he stops pouring. He has a  funny look on his face.

"Billie," he says slowly.
"Did you move your
project last night?"

Billie spins around.
Baby Noah is sitting on
the kitchen floor. He
has a big grin on his face.
Poking out of his mouth
is a popsicle stick with
a bit of pipe cleaner
stuck to it.

"The tower!" Billie and her dad shout together.

Billie rushes into the family room. Popsicle sticks and pipe cleaners are everywhere!

Billie storms back to the kitchen. "Noah! You ruined my school project!" she shouts at her baby brother. Noah begins to cry.

"Oh, Billie, I'm very sorry," says her dad. "But we did tell you to move your project. Noah is too little to know not to touch your things."

Billie looks at the ground. She is **angry**, but she didn't mean to make Noah cry. Billie gives Noah a cuddle. He stops crying.

Billie's dad puts his arm around her. "How about we try to stick it back together?" he says.

But Billie shakes her head. It won't dry in time now. Today is the day they are making their city. She has to think of something else. And fast!

Just then, Noah holds out

his hand toward Billie.

In his fist are two bits

of pipe cleaner twisted

together.

It reminds her

of something.

Suddenly, Billie

has an idea.

A super-duper idea!

"Thanks, Noah!" she says.

Billie runs into the family room. "I'll be ready in five minutes!" she calls.

What do you think she is up to?

# Chapter Four

Soon Jack arrives to walk to school with Billie.

Billie walks into the kitchen. She is carrying something covered with a dish towel.

It is something tall and
bumpy.

"Is that your tower?"
says Jack.

"Nope," says Billie.  "I decided to make something different."

"What is it?" Jack asks.

"It's a surprise!" says Billie. "I'll show you when we get to school."

Billie has a big grin on her face. But her tummy is full of butterflies.

33

What if Miss Swan doesn't like her project? What if everyone laughs at her?

"OK, then," says Billie's dad. "Time to go!"

He drives Billie and Jack to school because they are running late.

Billie and Jack walk into the classroom.

Miss Swan is at her desk. Lola and her friends are there too. They are all looking at Lola's project.

Lola has made a hospital out of a big cardboard box. When you peek in the windows it has matchboxes for little beds and people made out of pipe cleaners.

It is perfect. Just like Lola.

Billie puts her project
on her desk. Her heart
is beating very fast.

She pulls off the dish towel.

Underneath is a very strange-looking thing made out of twisted pipe cleaners and popsicle sticks.

Jack looks puzzled.

Lola turns around.
When she sees Billie's project, she laughs loudly.

"What is *that*, Billie? It looks crazy!"

Lola's friends giggle.

But Billie just smiles **bravely**. "It's a sculpture!" She replies. She hopes Miss Swan is listening.

Miss Swan gets up from her desk.

She swishes toward Billie
in her long skirt.
Billie holds her breath.
Her heart jumps up
and down.

"A sculpture!" says
Miss Swan. She claps
and her bracelets **jingle**.
"What a marvelous idea!
I love it!"

Billie grins. She is almost
bursting with pride.

"Thank you, Miss Swan," she says. "I got the idea from a book about Paris. In Paris there are sculptures *everywhere!*"

"You are absolutely right, Billie," Miss Swan says. "Every great city needs art. We will put your sculpture right in the middle of our city!"

Lola frowns.

Miss Swan leans in closer to look at Billie's crazy sculpture. "My goodness, this must have taken you ages," she says. "Did you have some help?"

"Um, yes, actually." Billie looks at Jack and giggles. "My baby brother helped me!"

43

# Collect them all!

Billie B. Brown

The Bad Butterfly

By Sally Rippin

Billie B. Brown

The Soccer Star

By Sally Rippin

Billie B. Brown

The Midnight Feast

By Sally Rippin

Billie B. Brown

The Second-best Friend

By Sally Rippin

Billie B. Brown

The Extra-special Helper

By Sally Rippin

Billie B. Brown

The Beautiful Haircut

By Sally Rippin

Billie B. Brown

The Big Sister

By Sally Rippin

Billie B. Brown

The Spotty Vacation

By Sally Rippin

Billie B. Brown

The Birthday Mix-up

By Sally Rippin

Billie B. Brown

The Secret Message

By Sally Rippin

Billie B. Brown

The Little Lie

By Sally Rippin

Billie B. Brown

The Best Project

By Sally Rippin

Billie B. Brown

The Deep End

By Sally Rippin

Billie B. Brown

The Copycat Kid

By Sally Rippin

Billie B. Brown

The Night Fright

By Sally Rippin